Paul

4-30/

P$ 306

8

Hank's
book

THE
Magic
Whistle

Weekly Reader Children's Book Club
presents

THE
Magic
Whistle

by Martha C. King

IVES WASHBURN, INC., NEW YORK

To my husband, Frank,
who still remembers
what it's like
to be ten years old.

✦✦ Contents ✦✦

THE
Magic
Whistle

CHAPTER

✦✦ I ✦✦

The Present

"Are you going to Miss Kat's birthday party?" Doug asked.

"A party for a cat? How silly can you get? That's even sillier than 'kid stuff'," Rod said.

"Well, I don't think it's silly if the games are fun, and if you get ice cream," Doug said. "Last year you thought the party was a great idea."

"That was last year when I was only nine. This is THIS year."

Rod looked at Doug's new bike and crammed his hands into his pockets to keep from reaching out and touching the shiny chrome handle bars. He mustn't show how much he wanted a bike. He must keep pre-

1

tending he'd rather roller skate. He kicked a rock into the street. The truth was he hadn't even been invited to Miss Kat's birthday party.

"Mrs. Tripp's an old fool," he said.

"Having a birthday party for an old cat! How silly can you get?" he went on. "Mrs. Tripp talks to Miss Kat like she's a real person, and she brushes her fur every day." Rod tried to keep his mind off the fact that Friday was *HIS* birthday, too, and this year he guessed he wasn't going to have a party. Nobody at home had said anything about his birthday, and he was sure they'd all forgotten. Mom and Dad were worried because nobody was working at the plant. Nobody was working because of the strike.

Rod watched Doug wet his finger with spit and polish the front fender of his bike.

"Don't you talk to your dog?" Doug asked.

Rod nodded.

"And don't you give him baths?"

Rod nodded again.

"Well, my mom says that's the same thing," Doug said.

"But Mrs. Tripp's a grown woman, and grown women don't talk to cats," Rod insisted.

"My mom says it's because Mrs. Tripp doesn't have any children of her own, and she likes kids," Doug explained.

Rod stared at the toe of his right sneaker and absentmindedly rolled a small stone around under its sole. "Yeah," he said.

Doug took his hands off the shiny chrome handlebars of his bike, put them up in the air, and shrugged his shoulders. "Sooo, since she likes kids so much, she wants to give us ice cream. Nothing wrong with that. You'd better think it over, Rod, and come to the party." He rode away. Rod watched him give a right-hand turn signal and go around the corner.

Rod knew the signals well. He'd learned them from a booklet passed out at school to bike owners. That was when he thought he was getting a bike for his birthday. He could still shut his eyes and feel himself riding through the wind, turning corners, and waving to a policeman who was smiling because here was a boy who'd learned his bike rider's manual.

Today, imagining didn't make him happy. Instead, he hurt in the pit of his stomach, especially when he remembered the family conference they had last night after dinner.

"Have some more coffee, dear?" Mom had asked Dad.

"No, thanks," Dad had said. "Lately I think coffee's been keeping me awake at night."

Mom opened her eyes wide and shook her head,

the way she always did when she didn't believe a word you'd said. Dad looked miserable and stared down at his cup and saucer.

"How long do you think the strike will last, Ed?" Mom asked in her quiet way, as if she wanted to hug you and kiss you on the forehead, but she didn't dare.

Dad shook his head and looked worried. "I wish I knew. Oh, how I wish I knew."

"Angie, would you like to be excused from the table?" Mom asked.

"Yes," Angie answered. "A button is falling off Googah's shirt. I'll have to sew it back on." And she disappeared into the hallway.

Mom shook her head and grinned. "That dilapidated, stuffed clown takes the place of a doll. She's put her other dolls away because she thinks she's too old to play with them." Then Mom looked toward Rod. "Now, I think we'd better have a family conference."

Rod's insides gave a little jerk. A family conference always meant he had to understand something unpleasant like maybe he and Dad couldn't go fishing on Saturday. When nice things were to be decided, Mom called it a family talk. Family talks were fun, but not family conferences. Besides, it must be serious if Angie was sent to play in another room. Angie was only eight.

Dad put the palms of his hands on the edge of the dining table, pushed himself straight in his captain's chair, and took a deep breath. "Rod, you know the men are on strike at the plant."

"Yes," Rod said.

"And you know I haven't been able to get a job to tide us over until work begins again?"

Rod nodded.

Dad leaned forward, put his elbows on the table. "You see, son, expenses go on—strike or no strike. We have to buy groceries, we have to make the house payment, and the payment on the boat. We'll have to be more careful with the money we've saved."

Rod looked straight into Dad's blue eyes, and felt safe and warm. No matter what happened, he knew Dad would take care of them.

Dad kept on talking. "In view of all this, son, it might be a good idea to sell the boat."

Rod began shaking his head.

"Wait. There's one more thing I have to say."

Rod shook his head harder.

"Some things we've planned on, we'll have to file away for another year. Like the bike you want."

"No, Dad! No! I gotta have that bike! I just gotta have it! I'm counting on it," Rod said, tears welling up in his eyes. He pushed his chair back quickly, stumbled from the table, up the stairs, and into his room.

A dog barked across the street and made Rod remember it wasn't last night. Why did Dad have to go on strike just when he was going to get his bike? Hadn't he waited two years for it already? It wasn't fair. He wanted to hit something, so he threw a rock toward the dog across the street. He felt ashamed of himself as the animal ran away, its tail between its legs. His own dog, Alexander, rubbed against his shoulder, and Rod put his arms around the collie's neck.

Mrs. Tripp came out of her front door and walked across the street toward him. He hoped she hadn't seen him throw the rock.

"Rod," Mrs. Tripp said, "I'm having a birthday party for Miss Kat, and I want you to come as usual. The time is Friday right after school. Remember, don't buy a present. Miss Kat had much rather have something you make for her yourself."

"Th-thank you, Mrs. Tripp," Rod managed to say.

"I know you're too old for things like this, Rod, but if you'll come, I promise you'll have a good time. Can I count on you?"

"I'll come, Mrs. Tripp," he promised.

Mrs. Tripp rang Rod's doorbell. Mom answered

the door and invited her in. Rod sat on the damp grass with Alexander and played mumbley peg with his jackknife. If he caught cold and died, it wouldn't matter that he wasn't getting a bike for his birthday. After a few minutes, Mrs. Tripp came out of the house and crossed the street to her own home. Rod felt warm fingers over his eyes.

"Guess who," Mom said, and she ruffled his hair because he was too big to be kissed in public. He wondered why she seemed so happy all of a sudden.

"What're you going to make for Miss Kat's birthday present?" she asked.

"I hadn't thought about it," Rod said.

"Well, you'd better start thinking because Friday is just two days away."

"I don't feel like making a birthday present for Miss Kat," Rod said.

Mom caught him by the hands and pulled him up to stand and face her. "Sometimes we have to hide our feelings and do what we're supposed to do just the same," she said, and she ruffled his hair again.

Why, he was almost as tall as Mom! He was always proud when anyone told him he looked like Mom. Soon he'd be old enough to take care of her when Dad went on strike.

"What about a scratching post? Miss Kat would

like that. Couldn't you use a piece of fireplace wood, tack some old carpet around it, and nail it to a square piece of board for a base?"

"I guess so," Rod said. "I'll try, anyway."

Mom went into the house humming a little tune. Rod hadn't seen her so happy since the strike began. He'd better get busy on that scratching post.

He found a short log of firewood about six inches in diameter and was sawing off the end to make it even, when he heard the doorbell ring. Giggling girls, he said to himself. And Mom was bringing them right out to the garage where he was working. They'd come to see Angie. Why didn't they stay out of his way? Angie was always bothering him, too. He wished he had a little house all to himself in the back yard. He'd live out there, and he'd put up a sign that said *NO GIRLS ALLOWED. SISTERS EITHER.*

"Hi, Rod!" Janie said.

"Are you coming to Miss Kat's birthday party?" Annette asked.

"What do you think I'm making? A merry-go-round?" Rod asked, irritated.

"What are you making, Rod?" Janie questioned.

"It's a scratching post for Miss Kat," Rod said. Girls didn't know anything. He had to waste time

telling them everything. Mom was a girl once, but he bet she was never as stupid as this.

"See you at the party," Annette said, after both girls had examined the scratching post and made silly suggestions. Perfume on a scratching post! Who ever heard of such a thing?

The girls went away giggling. Why did all girls have to act as if they knew a secret? And why did they have to giggle so much?

Angie came skipping back to the garage, her honey-colored pony tail flipping from side to side. "I know a secret! I know a secret!" she sang.

"Angie," Mom called from the kitchen, "secrets aren't to be told, and from the way you're acting, I don't think you'll have one very long. Come help me set the table and leave your brother alone."

Mom and Dad were especially cheerful at dinner.

"This is good hamburger, Sweetie," Dad said to Mom.

A smile spread over Mom's face like the sun coming out on a cloudy day. The corners of her eyes crinkled up, and her nose gave a little twitch. Rod liked to see Mom smile this way. It was almost as though the strike had never been. Maybe Dad found out work would begin soon at the plant. Maybe even before Christmas.

"Rod made something nice this afternoon, Ed. After dinner, you two might like to go out in the garage and look it over."

Dad smiled proudly at Rod, and Rod smiled back. It was almost like old times, before the strike.

"It's a scratching post for Miss Kat," Rod said. "It's her birthday."

Rod thought he saw a secret look pass between Mom and Dad. Neither of them seemed to think it was silly for Miss Kat to have a birthday party. Angie helped clear the plates away, and Mom brought in dishes of apple pie. It was swell for Uncle Jim to bring the apples from the ranch.

There was no blue cheese this time. Rod guessed blue cheese cost too much money with the strike going on.

"Ah, just enough cinnamon," Dad said. He made an "O" with his thumb and forefinger, winked his eye, and gave a little click out of the corner of his mouth.

"Rod," Mom said. "Angie's helping Mrs. Tripp get ready for the party. She won't have time to make a toy for Miss Kat. Would you mind letting the scratching post be from both of you?"

Rod put down his fork full of pie and looked up quickly. "I made it myself, and I'm giving it. Let

Angie give Miss Kat something else." He began eating his pie again.

"I'm asking you to share it," Mom said.

"But, Mom," Rod wailed.

Dad cleared his throat. "And I'm telling you to share it."

Rod frowned. "But I made it all by myself."

Dad's face was stern. Rod knew there was no use arguing. "O. K. O. K. I'll let Angie give it with me, but I don't want to."

After school on Friday, Rod and Angie crossed the street to Mrs. Tripp's and rang the doorbell. Rod carried the present. They were the last to arrive at the party because they hadn't been able to find a piece of tissue paper large enough to wrap the scratching post.

"I have an idea," Mom had said. "I'll just iron out this old piece of ribbon, and we'll make a big bow and pin it to the top of the scratching post. That'll do the trick. It doesn't have to be wrapped."

Mrs. Tripp answered the doorbell. Miss Kat was sitting in the middle of a ring of children, blinking her big green eyes. She had a bow of ribbon on her neck that almost matched the one on top of the scratching post, and Rod knew their present was just right. For the first time in two days, he felt happy.

"We'll play the games in the back yard," Mrs. Tripp said. "I'm glad the weather is warm and sunny."

During the games, Rod was having such a good time he forgot about thinking a party for a cat was silly. He forgot he'd said Mrs. Tripp was an old fool. In fact, he forgot everything except that he was having a wonderful time.

"Into the dining room for ice cream and cake," Mrs. Tripp called from the back door. As Rod passed by, she touched him on the shoulder and said, "Thank you for leading the games. I'm glad you're getting to be such a grown-up young man."

There were candles on the cake, ten to be exact. Rod thought Miss Kat was thirteen, but he guessed Angie'd counted wrong. Mrs. Tripp got Miss Kat from under the bed, and everybody began to sing *HAPPY BIRTHDAY*. When they came to the place where they were to say whose birthday it was, Rod sang, "Happy birthday, Miss Kat", but everybody else sang, "Happy birthday, dear Roddy. Happy birthday to you."

All the children squealed and laughed. So that was the secret! Doug gave him a friendly hit on the shoulder, and Mrs. Tripp said, "Well, Rod, make your wish, blow out the candles, and open your presents. The eating can wait."

Rod blew out the candles, every one with one blow, and the other guests said, "Ahhhhh!"

"Now make a wish," Angie said.

Rod closed his eyes tightly. He'd pretend he was making a wish. He didn't dare wish for anything he knew he wouldn't get, like a bike. It was foolish to make a wish that couldn't possibly come true.

"Now, open your presents, Rod," Mrs. Tripp said.

He opened the presents slowly, untying each ribbon as if it were a prized possession. There were socks, games, marbles, and polished rocks. The last present was from Dad. So he knew about the party all along!

When he pulled the wrappings apart to see what could be in such a small package, there on the white tissue paper, looking every bit as shiny as a star was *THE SILVER WHISTLE.*

"The whistle!" Angie gasped. "You finally got it!"

Rod felt sick for a minute. He'd wanted the whistle for so long. Dad won it in high school for being best-all-around athlete. But now that Rod had it, he couldn't feel happy. It reminded him of the shiny chrome on the bike he was supposed to have gotten for his birthday.

"I guess your folks'll give you the bike tonight, huh, Rod?" Doug asked.

Rod drew a quick little breath. He'd bragged so much to Doug about the promised bike. He had to say something, and fast.

"Bike?" he said, as he swallowed a big lump in his throat. "Oh, I don't think I'll want a bike now. I'll be doing so many things with this whistle, I'll be too busy to bother with a bike. It might even be a magic whistle. See? It has Dad's name engraved right here. *EDWARD R. BAINES*. The R's for Roderick. Same as my name. Now the whistle belongs to me."

He'd said something without showing how badly he hurt on the inside!

✦✦ II ✦✦

The Boat

Bright sunshine pried open Rod's eyes. For some reason he didn't feel happy. His right hand closed over something hard and cold under his pillow. *THE SILVER WHISTLE!* He rolled over on his back and held it in both hands, high, with his arms outstretched, to see it better. The metal caught a beam of sunlight and bounced it into Rod's sleepy eyes. What if it were a magic whistle like he'd said at the party?

He brought it closer to the end of his nose and stared at it hard. Dad said if silver were absolutely smooth, it'd look black. Millions of little scratches on it made silver reflect the light and look bright. Rod tried to see the scratches, but he couldn't find a single one. He'd examine the whistle under the microscope at school on Monday. Doug'd want to see the scratches, too.

Now that the whistle was his, he was going to wear it around his neck on the red, white, and blue plastic lanyard he'd made in cub scouts last summer. As he held the whistle in the air, the dangling lanyard swung back and forth across his nose, slightly touching it with each swing.

He remembered the times Mom used to let him take the whistle out of her cedar chest to look at it. He'd ask if he could blow it just once, and she'd say yes.

"When may I have it for my very own?" he'd ask.

And she'd say, "When you're old enough not to lose it."

And Angie'd say, "I want it."

And Mom'd say, "No, Angie, it's Rod's. It has his name on it."

Alexander stirred in his bed in the corner and made Rod stop remembering. Maybe he'd teach Alexander to do tricks by the whistle, and they could have shows in the back yard on Saturdays. Rod didn't know exactly how to train a dog, but maybe he could find somebody who could tell him. He closed his eyes and imagined the sign he'd put on the back gate.

ONLY FIVE CENTS TO SEE
THE TRAINED DOG PERFORM
HURRY BEFORE ALL TICKETS
ARE SOLD

Maybe he could save enough for a bike. It'd take a long time, but he could try.

Rod smelled the coffee Mom was making for break-fast, and he heard her opening and closing the refrig-erator door. In a few minutes she'd call him to get up.

The telephone rang, and he heard Dad answer it. He lay still and turned the whistle from side to side, watching the mischievous sun play hide and seek with its magic flashes. He could make the flashing light hit the wall and walk, in jerks, up to the ceiling. On the inside he felt more certain than ever that the whistle was magic, too.

"Rod, boy," Dad called from the living room downstairs, "hurry and get dressed. I've a message for you."

"Right away, Dad," Rod answered.

He dressed as quickly as he could and hung the whistle around his neck. The lanyard was too long, so he dropped the whistle into his shirt pocket, as his gym teacher did at school. Then, he took it out of his shirt pocket and blew it softly, just once. After breakfast, he'd go skating and blow it as loudly and as much as he wanted.

At the sound of the whistle, Alexander cocked his ears. His eyes laughed, and he stood very still. "Right after breakfast, Alexander, we'll go skating and blow the whistle some more," Rod promised.

Whistling a little tune, Rod checked his pockets to be sure he had all the necessary equipment he might need during the day. His jackknife, a good nail, a long piece of heavy string without knots in it, and a piece of wire coiled into a neat little ring. Then he patted his pocket again to be sure his whistle was still where it ought to be, stumbled down the stairs, three steps at a time, holding on to the bannister. His new school shoes seemed much too long for the width of the steps this year.

Rod sat down in his chair at the table, and Mom put a plate with egg and toast in front of him. "How's my birthday boy?" she asked.

"Gee, Mom, I sure was surprised when they sang *HAPPY BIRTHDAY* to me. I thought it was Miss Kat's party all the time, up until then."

Angie scrunched up her shoulders and grinned. "We had it all planned. Everybody knew except you. It was hard to keep from telling."

"I know," Mom said. "You almost told once, but I stopped you."

"Mrs. Tripp planned it, straight from the time I told her Rod couldn't have a party this year because of the strike."

Rod took a fork full of egg, chewed, and swallowed it. "What was the message Dad had for me, Mom?"

Dad came in the back door rubbing the palms of his hands together. "It's chilly this morning, but I think we'll have a nice warm day, anyway. Should be comfortable out in the boat."

Rod held his breath. Maybe Dad isn't going to sell the boat, after all, he thought.

"Rod," Dad said, "do you know a Mr. Chaney down at the Olsen Apartments?"

"Yes, Dad. I talk to him lots of times when he's working in the yard. He takes care of the apartments. He thinks Alexander's a keen dog."

"Mr. Chaney called this morning. Wants you to help him as soon as you've finished your breakfast. Sprained his ankle, and wants you to walk a dog for him."

"O. K. What dog?" Rod asked. He already had a real use for his whistle!

"I can't tell you that. He didn't say. Hurry and eat. He wants you there by seven-thirty."

"Don't gulp," Mom said.

"O. K., Mom. Thanks again for the whistle, Dad."

Rod drank the last of his milk and excused himself from the table. "It's like this, Alexander," he explained. "I know I said I'd take you with me this morning, but I have to walk another dog, and the other dog might not want you around. On the other hand, you might not want the other dog around, either. See what I mean?" Alexander licked Rod's hand and seemed to understand. Rod gave him a head-ruffle.

Once outside, he took the whistle out of his shirt pocket, inhaled deeply, and blew a long shrill blast. Alexander barked from inside the door. Yes, sir, Rod thought, as he put on his skates, Alexander was going to like the whistle.

When he reached the Olsen Apartments, Rod wondered if he'd be able to find Mr. Chaney's office without any trouble. He opened the back hall door and looked for some basement steps. Then, the first door on the right opened. Mr. Chaney hobbled out, using a cane. His ankle was tightly bound with an elastic bandage.

"A sprained ankle along with rheumatism doesn't help much if you've a lively dog to walk every day," he said to Rod. "You'll find Mrs. North's dog leashed to the doorknob outside her apartment on the second floor."

Rod's heart skipped a beat. "You mean the Witch of the North's dog?"

Mr. Chaney looked puzzled. "The 'Witch of the North's' dog?" he asked.

"That's what the guys at school call her."

"That isn't very kind of them, you know. She's a nice lady."

"They say nobody's seen her in twenty years," Rod said. "Not even through her windows. They say she's there all right, but she makes herself invisible."

Mr. Chaney pointed his finger at Rod. "Now that's how stories get exaggerated. Her sister comes to visit her every year. Comes all the way from Alaska."

"Have you ever been in her apartment to fix things?" Rod asked.

"Yes, I have. Neat and old-fashioned as you please. Smells like lavender."

"Why won't she let anybody see her?"

"Now, I'd say that's her business. Apartment's at the head of the stairs. You go get the dog. Name's Nancy Hanks. Born on February 12th, Lincoln's birthday, so Mrs. North named her for Lincoln's mother. When you bring Nancy Hanks back from her walk, hang the leash on the doorknob, ring the bell, and leave right away. Understand?" Mr. Chaney said.

Rod nodded and tip-toed quietly up the steps. The pounding of his heart sounded like a giant pump. So the Witch of the North had a dog. Could it be that little black one he'd seen Mr. Chaney walking a few days ago? Witches usually had cats, not dogs, didn't they? He sniffed the air. Something smelled good, like ladies' perfume, maybe. The smell grew stronger as he climbed the stairs. He knew Mr. Chaney wouldn't tell him a lie, but he couldn't help remembering the weird stories he'd heard about the Witch of the North. Rod felt as if he were being pushed toward a big hot oven to be baked like gingerbread.

His heart pumped louder as he climbed nearer to the top of the stairs, but the sight of the little black Manchester terrier almost made him forget his fright. She didn't wag her tail. She wagged her whole hind end. Rod wondered how the front end of her ever stayed hooked on to her back end.

Nancy Hanks seemed to know he'd come to take her for her walk, and she was in a hurry to get started. Rod let her lead him out of the apartments, and down the street. Doug rode by on his bicycle. "Whose dog?" he asked.

"Mrs. North's," Rod said.

"You mean the Witch of the North's dog?" Doug turned his bike around and pedaled slowly back toward Rod.

"The same."

"Aren't you afraid?"

"Naw, why should I be afraid?" Rod straightened his shoulders and felt very brave.

"I would. I'd sure be afraid," Doug said. "Wait until the other guys hear about this." And he rode away.

Nancy Hanks was the busiest little dog Rod had ever seen. She sniffed at everything, even the flowers.

"Look out for bees, Nancy Hanks," Rod warned.

Nancy Hanks followed with her nose the travels of a large black ant down the sidewalk. She nuzzled and barked at a slug making its shiny path from one flower bed to another. The slug drew himself up into a little round lump. A bird was hopping nervously from one limb of a bush to another. Nancy Hanks stalked it like a hunting dog. And she liked the whistle.

When the walk was over, and the two had climbed the stairs to Mrs. North's apartment, Rod looped the end of the leash over the doorknob and rang the bell. "You're a neat little dog, Nancy Hanks," he said. "I like you a lot. I just hope you don't wag your hind end off your front end before I see you again."

Rod remembered Mr. Chaney said "ring the bell and leave right away", but as he started down the stairs, he thought of stopping on the landing and taking a peek at Mrs. North. She'd have to come out to get Nancy Hanks. Something inside him said "no". Everyone is entitled to his own privacy, Mom always said. Rod stumbled down the stairs, three steps at a time, holding on to the bannister. When he reached the bottom step, he heard Mrs. North open her door and say to Nancy Hanks, "Come in, baby. Did you have a nice walk?" She didn't sound like a witch at all.

Rod went by Mr. Chaney's office to report the job completed.

"Do you think you could walk Nancy Hanks all next week?" Mr. Chaney asked Rod.

"I'd like that," Rod said. "See you at seven-thirty in the morning."

"Wait, Rod. That means after school, and again at eight-thirty at night. Think you can do it?"

"I'll ask my mom and dad," Rod said, "but I'm almost sure I can. The street lights make it bright as day at night. I'll let you know as soon as I get home. I'll telephone you."

"Good enough," Mr. Chaney said.

Rod put on his skates and started for home. The weather'd be fine for a boat ride today, he thought happily, as he looked up at the sunny sky. He took the whistle out of his pocket and blew it softly so Nancy Hanks wouldn't hear it. If he was going to train Alexander and Nancy with the whistle, he must blow it only when he was about to give a command.

Alexander had such a big mouth and such a long tongue you felt he was going to lap you up with one lick when he greeted you at the door. "Ready to go for a ride in the boat, Dad," Rod called, after Alexander had finished his juicy greeting.

Dad came into the living room. He looked worried. "Come over here and sit beside me, Rod. I want to talk to you."

Dad acted as if he couldn't find the right words to say. He rubbed his forehead with the tips of his fingers as if he had a headache. "Son, I might as well come straight to the point. I had a good chance to sell the boat this morning."

"No, Dad! No! We're going fishing this afternoon," Rod cried, finding it hard to hold back the tears.

"Now, wait and let me explain before you decide how you feel about this. You know we bought the boat second-hand, and we got a good buy. This morning, I had a chance to sell it for exactly what we paid for it, without losing a cent, even for equipment. I mightn't have had a chance like that again. So, to get the payments off my back, I sold the boat." Dad put his arm around Rod's shoulders.

"I'm looking to the future, Rod," Dad went on. "Just this morning I was talking to some of the men I work with, and it looks like we're in for a long, hard pull. We probably won't get back to work for several months. We have to keep the house, and we have to eat right now, but we'll get another boat some day. I give you my word of honor."

Rod sat on the edge of the couch and faced Dad. "You gave me your word of honor about the bike, too," he said.

Dad didn't say anything. He just sat there, looking miserable. Rod raced up the stairs to his room, fighting to hold back the tears.

✦✦ III ✦✦

The Steady Job

A week of walking Nancy Hanks had eased the pain about the boat and not getting a bike for his birthday but now Rod faced a new problem. Tonight was the last night he'd be following the little black dog on her accustomed paths. He mustn't let anybody know how sad he felt.

"Mom, may I have some cookies in a plastic bag?" he asked.

"You certainly may. How many is some?"

"Oh, six or seven. I've taught Nancy Hanks to carry things in her mouth, and I thought I'd have her take Mrs. North some cookies. Mrs. North must be awful lonesome up there all by herself."

"In that case, I'll make it eight," Mom said.

"Mom, do you really think she could be a witch?"

"A witch? Whatever gave you that idea?"

"The kids call her a witch."

Rod knew there was really no such thing as a witch, but it was fun to make believe. It was the kind of fun that made goosebumps pop up all over you, same as on Halloween. "They say she makes herself invisible and stands inside her window when the kids come home from school. If you look up at her, she'll put a spell on you."

"Has she ever put a spell on you?" Mom asked.

"No, because we won't look up."

Mom winked at Dad. "Do you know anyone she's put a spell on?"

"No, but she can do it," Rod explained.

Rod climbed the stairs, two steps at a time, and went into his room. He wasn't sure he should put a date on the note, but it wouldn't hurt any. Maybe Mrs. North didn't know what date it was, living up there all by herself. Maybe she didn't even have a calendar. He made himself comfortable at his desk and began to write.

September 10

Dear Mrs. North,

I am sorry this is the last time for me to take Nancy Hanks for her walk. I like her a lot. She is a real fun dog. I have taught her to carry things in her mouth, so I am sending these cookies to you by her. You and Nancy Hanks can have a tea party. You must be awful lonesome up there by yourself all the time.

Respectfully,
Rod

He folded the note and stuffed it into an envelope. He wouldn't seal it because it wasn't polite to send a sealed note by anyone. He went downstairs to pick up the cookies. Maybe Mr. Chaney'd bring Nancy Hanks by to see him sometimes when he was taking her for a walk.

"She's almost as good as a personal friend, Mom," Rod said. He pushed Alexander back inside the house and closed the door behind him. He'd spend more time with Alexander next week.

Nancy Hanks was waiting, as usual, just outside Mrs. North's apartment. Her leash, as usual, was looped over the door knob. Rod knelt down on one knee and hugged the little black dog around the neck. Nancy Hanks stood on her hind legs and licked his ear.

"Well, let's go, girl," he said. "And stop wagging your hind end so hard. You might fall apart. I'd hate to have you fall apart the last time I take you for a walk. That wouldn't speak very well for me, now would it, girl?" He blew his whistle softly, and Nancy Hanks trotted beside him down the stairs.

As they passed by Mr. Chaney's door, the old man called out, "I want to see you when you get back, Rod. You have to pick up your pay envelope, too."

Funny, Rod thought. He'd been having such a good time he'd forgotten all about being paid. Walking a dog three times a day took a lot of time. He'd been too busy to think about money. He wondered what Mr. Chaney wanted.

Nancy Hanks led Rod out into the night. Dark came early in the fall of the year, but the street lights made the outside almost as bright as day. The little black dog was her usual, happy, curious self. That's the difference between dogs and people, Rod thought.

Nancy Hanks yipped at two big dancing lights between Annette's and Janie's houses. The girls were playing on the lawn with flashlights. The street light would've made the yard bright enough for horsing around, Rod thought. Girls were idiots, anyway.

"The witch's dog!" Janie squealed. "Run! Run!"

"Don't let that dog near me!" Annette yelled. "She'll put a spell on me!"

Rod pointed a finger at the girls just like Mr. Chaney had pointed at him. "Now, that's the way stories get exaggerated," he said in the same tone of voice Mr. Chaney used. "Nancy Hanks is a plain Manchester terrier. Maybe a little smarter than most, but she can't put a spell on you. Anyway, she wouldn't if she could. She's the nicest dog I know, not counting Alexander."

The girls came closer. Rod knelt down and let Nancy Hanks lick his ear. "See what a nice dog she is?" he said. "Nancy Hanks loves everybody. Would you like her to lick your ears? It tickles real funny."

Annette and Janie came even closer. In a minute, they were taking turns hugging Nancy Hanks and letting her lick their ears. The flashlights were lying on the grass with their lights still shining.

"She's a real nice dog, Rod. But aren't you afraid the Witch of the North'll put a spell on you just the same?" Janie asked.

Rod straightened his shoulders. He liked the girls to think he was brave. "Naw," he said. "I'm too smart to let her put a spell on me."

"How can you stop her?" Annette asked.

"I don't let her see me," Rod boasted. The truth was, Mrs. North wouldn't let him see her. He felt sheepish. Anyway, he'd straightened things out for

Nancy Hanks, and he felt good about that. There'd be plenty of time later to tell everybody Mrs. North wasn't a witch. Besides, he wasn't sure about it himself.

The girls began walking toward their houses. "I'm glad we found out Nancy Hanks is such a nice dog," Janie said, looking back over her shoulder.

"We like her a lot," Annette added.

Rod blew his whistle, and Nancy Hanks led him on down the street. She was a funny dog, Rod thought, always sniffing, listening, and barking. Sometimes he could hear and see what was making her bark, and sometimes he couldn't. Rod shut his eyes. Night sounds were nice to hear. Night air was good to smell. Maybe she barked sometimes because she was glad to be a dog, walking along a street at night, just sniffing, listening, and barking.

Back upstairs, it was really time to say goodbye to Nancy Hanks. "I'll see you once in a while," Rod promised. "I'll ask Mr. Chaney to bring you over to my house to play with Alexander and me. Alexander'll like you. I know he will. He's a big collie dog, and he might make you think he'll swallow you up in one big gulp, but he won't. You'll like Alexander, too. Honest, you will." Rod blew his whistle. "Now, sit."

Nancy Hanks sat. Rod reached in his pocket and

took out the letter and the cookies. "Take this bag in your mouth," he said, "and give it to Mrs. North. Give it to Mrs. North. Understand?" Then he stumbled down the stairs, leaving a little black dog sitting outside a door, holding a bag of cookies with a note pinned to it in her mouth.

Rod stopped at Mr. Chaney's door. "You wanted to see me, Mr. Chaney?"

"Yes, Rod. Would you like a permanent job? I was wondering, since I'm so busy and my rheumatism is bothering me, if you'd like to keep on walking Nancy Hanks indefinitely?"

"Would I? Now I'll have a chance to train her with my new whistle. I'll be here at seven-thirty in the morning."

Rod turned to go, but Mr. Chaney said, "Wait, boy. You didn't collect your wages." He handed Rod an envelope.

Rod opened it. Inside was a new dollar bill and a fifty-cent piece. He'd save it all for his bike, he decided at once.

He whistled as he skated home. Plans for himself, Alexander, and Nancy Hanks tumbled over each other in his mind. He'd train the dogs together and have them in his backyard circus. All the neighborhood kids would come, and he'd sell tickets at the gate. Then he'd change into an animal trainer's costume, and he'd put on his dog act. He might need Mom to serve the refreshments.

When he turned into his own frontyard, Rod took off his skates as quickly as he could.

"Mom! Dad!" he called, as he pushed open his front door and stumbled over Alexander. "Mom. Dad. I've something to tell you."

Mom and Dad were sitting at the kitchen table. They were very quiet, and they looked worried. Rod stopped still in the doorway.

"What's the matter?" he asked.

"Rod, your Uncle Jim is coming by tomorrow. We thought Alexander'd have a lot of fun spending the winter at the ranch. He'd be a help to Uncle Jim."

"No, Mom. No! I could never spare Alexander."

"Then we'll have to tell you, Rod," Mom said. "We can't afford to feed Alexander on our food budget. He's a big dog. You have no idea how much it costs to feed him."

Rod knelt down and hugged Alexander's neck. "I won't let them take you, boy. I'll never let them take you away. I'll pay for Alexander's food myself, I was going to tell you. I have a steady job. I'll be taking Nancy Hanks for her walks from now on. I'll buy Alexander's food."

✦✦ IV ✦✦

Three Gold Letters

Big collies made good pillows, Rod thought, as he lay on the living room floor. He guessed he knew now what being thankful meant. Uncle Jim had come and gone, and old Alexander was still around. He reached back over his head and scratched Alexander's neck. It would take all the money he could make taking Nancy Hanks for her walks to buy Alexander's food, but Rod didn't mind at all. They were buddies, Alexander and he, and buddies should be together.

Rod turned over on his stomach and laid his face against the big collie's head. Alexander was warm and alive. He could lick your face. He could tag along. Or he could wait for you to come home.

"Rod," Mom said, "those socks are practically new, and there's a hole in each toe. How do you do it?"

"Gee, Mom, I don't know. Maybe they're too little for me. My feet're a lot bigger this year than they were last year."

Mom sighed. "You're probably right, at that. But socks are so expensive."

"I'm sorry, Mom," Rod said, scratching Alexander behind the ears, "I'll try to walk lighter from now on."

Mom wasn't smiling. "That might help," she said.

Rod twisted Alexander's ear thoughtfully. "What

does Angie do over at Mrs. Tripp's on Saturday, Mom?" he asked, ignoring his sister.

Angie was sitting on the floor. She'd made a puppet out of Googah with strings and safety pins, and she was making him dance for her while she hummed *PEGGY O'NEILL*. "Why don't you ask me? I'm right here."

"O. K. What do you do at Mrs. Tripp's on Saturday mornings?"

"Sometimes I run the vacuum. Sometimes I dust. Sometimes I run an errand. Mrs. Tripp says I'm her 'right hand man'."

"You're not a man," Rod said. "You're a girl."

"Silly, I know I'm a girl. That's just the way you say it."

Rod ran his forefinger around under Alexander's collar. "How much does she pay you?"

Angie tossed her head and made her honey-colored pony tail dance. "It isn't p'lite to ask how much a person makes." She made Googah bow from the waist.

"Angie's right," Mom said.

Dad came up from the basement. "I'll be leaving Monday to help your Uncle Jim on the ranch for a while. I'm going to depend on you kids to take care of your mother for me."

"We aren't going?" Angie asked.

"You have to stay here and go to school," Dad said.

"Gee, Dad, do you have to go?" Rod asked.

Dad nodded. Mom kept on with her darning, not looking up.

Rod was glad it was time to take Nancy Hanks for her walk. It gave him an excuse to get out of the house and be by himself. As he skated the four blocks to the apartments, he wished Dad didn't have to go away. Or he wished he, Mom, and Angie could go along.

It was fun living on the ranch. He knew, because he and Alexander spent two weeks there last summer. He'd like to live on a ranch all the time, but Dad'd rather be a machinist. Everybody was different, Rod guessed. When he grew up, he'd like to have a ranch like Uncle Jim. Then he'd have a horse, and he wouldn't need a bicycle.

Outside the apartments, Rod took off his skates and opened the heavy hall door. Nancy Hanks heard him come in and gave a sharp little bark of hello. Rod talked quietly to her as he climbed the stairs. "Nice girl. Nice girl," he said.

Nancy Hanks was never satisfied until she'd licked his ears in greeting. It was the same thing as saying she liked him, and he was her best friend. Rod didn't mind a bit. He wondered if she licked Mrs. North's ears, too, and if Mrs. North minded. He wondered if Mrs. North would ever open the door and talk to him. She must be an O. K. lady to have a dog like Nancy Hanks.

Rod blew his whistle softly, and the little black dog walked beside him down the stairs, up the hall, and out into the street.

"Let's walk toward my house for a change, Nancy Hanks," Rod said, and he blew his whistle along with a tug on the leash. Nancy Hanks turned around. She seemed glad to explore new territory.

As they passed the side of Mrs. Tripp's house, Nancy Hanks stopped and barked furiously. Miss Kat sat on the back fence, blinking her big green eyes. If it hadn't been for the street light, Rod couldn't have seen her, because Miss Kat was solid black, except for a little patch of white under her chin where a bow-tie ought to be.

"Can't you be friends with Miss Kat?" Rob asked.

Nancy Hanks continued to bark.

"Spptt," Miss Kat said.

Rod tugged at the leash. "No, I guess you can't. But if you'd take the trouble to get to know each other, you could be friends, good friends. We'll have to work on that."

Nancy Hanks didn't seem to be ashamed of herself. Instead, she seemed delighted she'd done her duty as a dog by barking at a cat. Rod blew his whistle. "O. K., Nancy Hanks. Let's go home."

After Rod had said goodnight to the little black dog, he went down the steps as quietly as he could, but Mr. Chaney heard him.

"Rod," the old man called.

Rod walked to the open door of Mr. Chaney's office. Mr. Chaney was working at his desk over a pile of papers. Why does a janitor have to work on so many papers? Rod wondered.

"I have something for you," Mr. Chaney said. "Let's see. It was right here on the desk under these bills." He fingered through a stack of papers, looking over his gold-rimmed glasses. "Yes, here it is. Right here where I put it, under all these bills. It's a note from Mrs. North. She asked me to give it to you."

Rod walked over to the desk and took the note. He held it for a minute, almost afraid to open it. A faint odor rose from the envelope. He brought it closer to his nose. It smelled like lavender, like Mr. Chaney said her apartment smelled. The same smell was in the apartment halls, too.

Rod took the note out of the envelope. The stationery was thin and pretty, and in the left hand top corner of the page were the letters *WON*, printed in gold. He began reading.

Dear Rod,

Thank you for the cookies. They were very good. Nancy Hanks and I had a party as you suggested.

Sincerely,

Mrs. North

Rod stared at the note. What did the large gold letters mean? Could they stand for Witch of North?

"Yes, Rod," Mr. Chaney said, without turning around.

Rod shuddered. How'd Mr. Chaney know he wanted to ask him something? "What do the letters WON stand for, Mr. Chaney?"

"WON stands for Wanda Olsen North," the old man said, without stopping his writing.

After a silent time had passed, Mr. Chaney said again, "Yes, Rod?"

"Th-these are the Olsen Apartments, aren't they?" Rod asked, almost as if he were talking to himself.

"Yes, they are. Mrs. North owns them."

"Owns them? She must be rich."

"No, she's not rich," Mr. Chaney said, "but she

has enough. Now is there anything else you want to ask?"

"No, sir."

As Rod went out into the crisp night air, he took a deep breath. He'd write Mrs. North a note and tell her to send the next letter by Nancy Hanks. It wouldn't matter if the envelope was a little wet and chewed up. If Mrs. North would come out, he'd show her how to make Nancy Hanks sit up and hold a note in her mouth. Of course, she'd have to buy herself a whistle.

+ + **V** + +

The Fair

The noisy old ton-and-a-half farm truck rattled down the highway toward Puyallup. Rod and Angie sat in the cab beside Uncle Jim. What luck, Rod thought! If the new truck had been ready today instead of tomorrow, Uncle Jim would be on his way back to the ranch right now, and he and Angie would be in school.

"I have a great idea," Uncle Jim had said to Mom last night. "Since the lettering won't be dry on the new truck until tomorrow, why don't I take Rod and Angie to the Puyallup fair? Several of my friends'll be there with their animals, and we could get in some good visiting."

"Yipee!" Rod yelled.

"Yes! Yes!" Angie squealed.

Mom slapped her hands together for attention. "Quiet down, you two. I haven't said you could go yet, and I don't like you to skip school." She looked at Uncle Jim. "You don't have children of your own, Jim. I wonder if you know what you're letting yourself in for?"

Uncle Jim ruffled Rod's hair and hugged Angie. "Oh, they won't be any trouble, will you, Rod?"

Rod shook his head, remembering the times at the ranch he forgot to listen to Uncle Jim.

"We'll be good," Angie said.

"Tee and I'll be parents pretty soon. I might as well get in practice."

Mom nodded. "Well, I guess the best way to learn about taking children to a fair is to take them." Uncle Jim grinned, and Mom continued, "It costs money to go to a fair, and I don't have any to spare."

"We'll spend most of our time looking at the animals and the farm exhibits," Uncle Jim said. "I might check the price of a new tractor, too."

Mom put on her figuring expression. "You say you have passes for the gate, Jim, and I could fix your lunch. I'll give the children money for one ride each." She looked at Rod and Angie. "You'll have to choose very carefully."

"Don't worry about lunch," Uncle Jim said. "We'll have a hamburger and an orange drink before we go to the rodeo."

"Now, Jim, that's too expensive. I can't let you buy them tickets for the rodeo."

Uncle Jim pretended to be indignant. "Will you let me spend what I please on my own niece and nephew?"

Just thinking about last night made Rod smile to himself. Yes, sir, Uncle Jim was an all right guy. Not as good as Dad, of course, but almost as good. Hadn't Uncle Jim walked back to the apartments with him late last night to ask Mr. Chaney if he'd take Nancy Hanks for her afternoon walk in Rod's place? Just like a dad. Uncle Jim explained about the new truck and the fair to Mr. Chaney, and Mr. Chaney understood right away.

Rod knew it'd been only nine days since Dad went to work at the ranch, but it seemed like a year. Uncle Jim promised he'd send Dad next time anyone had to come to Seattle on business. When you traded trucks, you had to sign papers. Dad couldn't sign Uncle Jim's name. Rod could understand that.

"I'm glad the tires on this truck are good," Uncle Jim yelled over the roar of the engine as they rode along next morning.

Rod nodded. It was easier to nod than to say anything with so much noise around.

Angie tapped Rod on the knee to get his attention. "Remember, no cotton candy, and no balloons. Mom said so."

"You're the one to remember that," Rod said. "I have to remember not to want to shoot at the targets in the shooting gallery."

There was no glass in the window on Rod's side of the truck. He pulled his jacket collar closer around his neck. Nobody said much during the rest of the twenty-six mile trip. Twice, Uncle Jim looked over at Rod and winked. After a long time, Rod saw the sign that said WELCOME TO THE CITY OF PUYALLUP, population 10,010.

"There're the fair grounds," Uncle Jim said, pointing to the right.

Rod looked. He could see the flags flying.

After they parked the truck, Rod walked proudly beside Uncle Jim toward the fair ground gate. He wished he could skip with Angie, but men didn't skip. It was hard taking the same-sized steps as Uncle Jim because Rod's legs were much shorter.

A minute later, Uncle Jim was showing his pass to the ticket-taker.

"How ya, Jim," the ticket-taker said.

"How ya, Bob," Uncle Jim said.

"You know him?" Rod asked surprised.

Uncle Jim nudged Rod's arm. "We ranchers get around."

The sound of music made Rod excited, and the smells of popcorn and hot dogs made him hungry. "What time is it, Uncle Jim?"

Uncle Jim looked at his watch. "Nine-thirty."

Rod swallowed hard. It'd be a long time until lunch, and he wondered if he could wait.

Suddenly, Uncle Jim stopped walking and turned around to face Rod and Angie. He put his right hand on Angie's left shoulder and his left hand on Rod's right shoulder. "Now, let's get organized. The rodeo's at two o'clock. We'll see the wildlife before we head for the live stock barns. I want to see a friend of mine on business. After that, we'll pick out the ride you like best. By then, I expect it'll be lunchtime."

"Lunchtime?" Rod's voice was small, and he swallowed hard.

Uncle Jim grinned. He stood up straight with his hands in his pockets. "Tell you what, kids. I think I could do with a little snack right now. Say an orangeade and a hot dog. That should hold us until noon."

"I could eat a horse and snap at the bridle," Rod said, imitating one of the cowboys on Uncle Jim's ranch.

Angie put both her hands over her stomach. "I'm starved."

Uncle Jim led the way to a lunchstand. The smell of hot dogs sizzling on a grill so close to him made Rod a little dizzy. He stopped to watch the chef turn ten frankfurters in one swing with the back of his fork, like Mom running the back of her fingernails over a whole octave of piano keys at once. The orangeade bubbling in the big upside-down jug made Rod think of fishing on the river with Dad.

"Tell him what you want on your hot dogs," Uncle Jim said to Rod and Angie, "and go over there and sit at the table."

Angie wanted mustard, and Rod wanted catsup, mustard, and onions. They sat at a table made out of new, unpainted wood, and there were fresh, clean wood shavings on the ground underneath.

Uncle Jim brought the hot dogs and the orange drinks.

"Uncle Jim, what would you say a hot dog tastes like?" Rod asked, chewing and turning his head a little to one side.

"Ummm, let's see," Uncle Jim said, taking a bite

and closing his eyes. "I'd say it tastes like—I'd say it tastes like— I give up. What would you say it tastes like, Rod?"

Rod closed his eyes and took another bite. "I'd say it tastes like—I'd say it tastes like—"

"The best thing in the world," Angie added quickly.

"You're right," Rod and Uncle Jim said together.

In the wildlife building, Rod spent so much time watching the otters he had to walk fast by all the other cages and pools. Then, Uncle Jim hurried them on to the cattle barn.

"Look around," Uncle Jim told them, "but don't wander out of my sight. At eleven-thirty, we pick out the rides."

When Angie and Uncle Jim found him after eleven-thirty, Rod was almost sorry. He was watching an older boy polish the horns and hoofs of a Jersey cow. The boy said his name was Bruce Manwaring, he was a member of the 4-H club, he'd raised the cow himself, her name was Cyd, and he hoped Cyd'd win a blue ribbon. It was funny to see a big animal like Cyd let her foot stay still in Bruce's lap while he polished her hoof. Cyd chewed her cud all the time Bruce was polishing, and she moved her head politely to one side when the wide brim of his western style hat brushed her face. She kept on chewing her cud while he polished her horns, too.

"I thought we were going to stay together," Uncle Jim said. "Now we'll have to miss the sheep and the rabbits."

The three of them walked and walked among the rides. Angie and Rod watched each ride carefully, trying to pick the best. Finally, they decided on the ferris wheel. They liked the one at the shopping center at home, and this one was bigger around and higher. Uncle Jim motioned toward the ticket office. "Buy your tickets," he said.

Rod rushed ahead of Angie, bought his ticket, and settled himself in one of the swinging seats. Angie bought her ticket and followed.

"You can't sit with me, Angie," Rod said.

"Sit together, kids," Uncle Jim called.

"No," Rod said. "This is the year Mom said I could ride by myself. I'm ten now."

Uncle Jim stood for a minute looking straight at Rod. Rod quickly busied himself adjusting the seat strap. Angie looked as if she might cry.

"If that's the way you feel about it, Rod, I don't think Angie wants to ride with you, either. I'll ride with you, Angie. Wait. I'll buy my ticket." Uncle Jim walked over to the ticket office.

"Jim Baines! What're you doing at the Western Washington Fair? I thought you took part in the Central Washington Fair."

"I do, Barney," Uncle Jim said. "Had to lay over in Seattle for a day waiting for a new truck. Thought I'd come down and look around. Brought my brother's kids with me."

He must know everybody, Rod thought, as he watched Uncle Jim and Angie get in the seat in front of him. The great wheel began to vibrate and turn slowly, gathering speed, taking the swinging seats backward to the top, over, and forward to the ground again. Each time Rod's seat went over the top, he wanted to say, "Hold on to your stomach, Angie", but Angie wasn't there to hear it. Uncle Jim began pointing out things on the fairgrounds to Angie. Rod listened as hard as he could, but he couldn't hear what Uncle Jim was telling her. It wasn't as much fun as he thought it'd be, riding in a seat all by himself.

As they left the ferris wheel behind them, Rod asked, "You know the ticket seller, too, Uncle Jim?"

"He brings his ferris wheel to the Yakima fair every year," Uncle Jim explained. "Spends his spare time hanging around the cattle barn."

Angie tugged at Uncle Jim's coat sleeve. "After we eat our lunch, what're we going to do?"

Uncle Jim stopped walking and pointed. "You see that grandstand up there? We're going to buy our rodeo tickets and go up there and sit until the show begins. You two can lie on the benches in the sun. We'll be sure of a good seat that way."

Rod hadn't planned on going to sleep on the bench in the grandstand. He'd intended only to shut his eyes and let the warm September sun shine down in his face, but the next thing he knew, Uncle Jim was shaking him, trying to get him to wake up. People were filling the grandstand, and they wanted good seats, too.

"Did Angie take a nap?" Rod asked, feeling a little silly because he'd gone to sleep.

"All three of us took a nap," Uncle Jim assured him.

At the other side of the parade ground, Rod could see the acts beginning to get in position. A few minutes later, the band began walking toward the grandstand, playing. The music made Rod wish he had a flag to wave. The master of ceremonies began to talk over the loud speakers, and the acts began to pass in parade. As each one came in front of the grandstand, it stopped to take a bow. The audience applauded. The band played a loud note. The clowns began teasing the children who had good seats down front.

One clown twisted a quarter out of Rod's nose, but he put the quarter in his pocket. He found another one behind Angie's ear.

After the grand entrance, the first act was three great brewery wagons drawn by eight big draft horses. They were followed by a miniature brewery wagon drawn by eight Shetland ponies. The audience cheered and clapped, especially for the driver of the Shetland ponies. Uncle Jim said it took a lot of skill to drive eight horses, and it took a lot of work to keep the horses and wagons looking good. They had to be kept looking like that all year, too. Not just at fair time. That meant a lot of work.

Next came the cowboys performing in the rodeo, roping calves, bulldogging, and riding bucking broncs and Brahma bulls. The clowns helped by drawing the attention of the bulls away from the fallen riders until they could scramble to safety.

Next came the acrobats. They walked tight ropes, swung on a trapeze, and stood on their heads on top of tall swaying poles. An animal trainer lead out a pony and a black dog.

Rod caught his breath. A trained dog! And a pony! That was just like Nancy Hanks and Alexander! Maybe he'd learn more about training Nancy Hanks and Alexander for the backyard circus.

The man with the pony and the dog was about to perform. When the band played one loud note, the pony put his right leg forward and bowed to the crowd. The dog stood on his hind legs. The audience cheered and clapped. The trainer blew his whistle and pointed to a small platform while the drummer beat his drums, louder and louder until the dog jumped to the platform. The trainer blew his whistle again, but this time he pointed to the pony's back. The drummer beat his drums again. The dog waited for the trainer's signal, then jumped up on the pony. Then the band played a tune, and the pony, with the dog standing on his back, trotted around the ring.

"That's neat!" Rod yelled, clapping his hands. "I wonder how he taught the dog to do that?"

"We'll ask him after the rodeo," Uncle Jim said.

"You mean it?" Rod asked, excitedly. "He's going off the field now. Let's meet him at the other end."

"Yes," Angie agreed.

"It might be a good idea, at that," Uncle Jim said. "We'll get out of here ahead of the crowd. The show's about over, anyway."

The three left the grandstand, Rod staying ahead of Angie and Uncle Jim. "Come on," he called back to them over his shoulder.

When they reached the other end of the field, the animal trainer was just going into the barn.

"Joe! Joe Polatty!" Uncle Jim called.

The animal trainer turned around. He held the pony's lead strap in one hand and the dog's leash in the other. "Jim Baines!" he said. "What're you doing here? Glad to see you."

Rod drew a quick little breath. This was too good to be true. Uncle Jim knew the animal trainer, too!

Uncle Jim shook hands with Joe. "I brought Ed's kids to the fair. Joe, this is Angie, and this is Rod." He turned to Rod and Angie. "This is Joe Polatty."

Joe offered his hand to Rod. "Shake hands with an old friends of your dad's."

"You know Dad?" Rod asked, more surprised than ever.

"The three of us used to play together on a ranch outside Wenatchee when we were boys," Joe said.

Uncle Jim grinned. "Rod wants to ask you something, Joe," he said.

"Ask away, Rod."

"I want to know how you trained your dog."

Joe smiled and made a sweeping gesture toward the pony. "First, let me introduce you to Shasta. Shasta, this is Rod. And this is Angie." Shasta put his right foot forward and respectfully lowered his head. Rod was delighted.

Joe gestured toward the dog. "And this is Trilby.

Trilby, shake hands with Rod." Trilby solemnly offered his paw. "Now, shake hands with Angie."
Trilby did.

"Rod, you asked me how I trained Trilby," Joe
continued. "First, you have to have patience. You
can't expect too much right at first. You have to give
the dog time to understand what it is you want him
to do. There's where the kindness comes in." He patted Trilby's head.

Rod already knew these things. Hadn't he taught
Nancy Hanks to sit up and hold things in her mouth?

Joe was talking again. "The next thing is signals. I
use a whistle to get the dog's attention. Then I use a
hand signal for what I want him to do. When I begin
the training, I pat the place I want him to jump. Later
I can point, and he'll understand. I raise my hand for
'up', and I lower my hand for 'down'. See what I
mean?"

Rod nodded.

"Then I give him a reward. A dog yummie, maybe.
I let the dog have time to learn one thing well before
I try to teach him something else. The box first, then
the pony's back."

Rod could hardly wait to get started home. He
had plans. Important plans.

✦✦ VI ✦✦

Backyard Circus

Dad had been working on the ranch for two weeks, and Rod had taken over as "man of the house". It was his job to go with Mom to the store and help her with her bags of groceries. He kept a check on the furnace in case the fall winds blew out the pilot light, and he saw that all the doors were locked at night. He missed Dad, but he was proud he was old enough to look out for Mom and Angie. Alexander was behaving better than usual, too. He'd stopped sleeping in Rod's room, and was keeping all-night watches by the front door. Rod wondered if the big collie knew something was wrong, and was trying to help. Good old Alexander! Angie and Mom sang a lot as they washed the dishes and made the beds. Mom said it kept "Old Man Gloom" away.

Rod didn't have to sing to keep "Old Man Gloom" away. He was too busy training Nancy Hanks and Alexander for the backyard circus he'd planned. Mrs. North sent a note by Nancy Hanks saying he could take the little black dog to his house every afternoon for a short lesson. Nancy Hanks learned fast, and Alexander was always eager to please. Doug was the only boy Rod allowed in the backyard to watch the training. When it was raining, Mom let them use Rod's bedroom for the circus ring.

"You see, Doug, you do it this way," Rod said, and he blew his whistle.

Nancy Hanks sat up on her hind legs at the sound of the whistle and the sight of an "up" hand-signal from Rod. He patted the top of the wooden box beside the wide back step. The dog jumped up nimbly and sat on the spot he'd patted.

"Nice girl. Nice girl," Rod said, as he held out a dog yummie to her. Nancy Hanks gobbled up her reward and was ready for more practice and more dog yummies.

Doug clapped his hands. "Neat, Rod. Real neat!"

"And that's not all, Doug. Next, I'm going to teach her to jump up on Alexander's back instead of the box. The animal trainer at the fair told me how to train her."

"That'll be great, Rod!" Doug said. "But do you think Alexander'll let Nancy Hanks jump up on his back?"

"Alexander? Why Alexander'll do anything I want him to do, won't you, boy?" Alexander wagged his tail and almost knocked Doug down. "Besides, you like Nancy Hanks, don't you, boy?" Rod asked, scratching the hair on the big collie's head.

"Say, Rod! I have some ruffles at home I had on an old clown suit. I'll bring them to put around the dogs' necks for costumes."

Rod looked at Doug thoughtfully. "Why can't you help me with the circus, Doug? I'll need a 'right-hand man'."

"You mean it, Rod? Sure, I'll help you."

In his mind, Rod could see the dogs with ruffles around their necks. Maybe Doug could help out in lots of ways. "I was thinking, Doug. Maybe I'll need a partner. I'll take care of the dog act. You can be a clown and take care of the tickets. Of course, it'll be my circus."

"That'd be fun, Rod. I'll ask my mom to make us some lemonade and cookies to sell. How's that?"

"You can borrow my record player for the music, Rod," Angie said from the doorway. "And Janie, and Annette, and I can dance for the circus."

Rod put his hands on his hips and said firmly, "No girls! We're not gonna have any girls around our circus!"

Mom came to the door and stood behind Angie. "Rod, do you remember the circus your father took you to last year?"

Rod kept looking down at the ground. "Yes, Mom."

"Do you remember coming back and telling me about the girls in the acts?"

"Yes, Mom."

"I think you'd better change your mind. I'll fix a costume for Angie, and she can be the 'dancing and music lady'. Yes?"

"No, I won't let her. If you make me have her in my circus, I just won't have a circus at all."

Angie didn't say anything. She turned and danced out the front door, letting it slam behind her.

Outside, Doug asked. "You really mean it, Rod? You won't have the circus if Angie's in it? We'll be missing a lot of fun."

Rod nodded, his lips pressed together, tight.

"I don't see why she can't be in it, Rod, as long as she's not in your dog act," Doug pleaded.

Rod put his hands in his pockets. He looked down at the toe of his right shoe and twisted himself from side to side. "Well, I guess you do have to have more'n one act in a circus. But don't forget, the dog act's the main event. Angie can dance after my dog act."

"I thought you always saved the best things for last, like dessert," Doug said. "I gotta be going." And he rode off on his bike.

Rod went back into the kitchen. Mom wasn't smiling. She looked sort of sad.

"I have to take Nancy Hanks home now," he said quickly, glad to be getting away. He couldn't stand to have Mom disappointed in him.

He felt sick on the inside as he put the harness on Nancy Hanks and hooked the leash to it. Once out in the street, he let the little black dog lead him back to the apartments. Doug passed by on his bike as Rod was about to push open the heavy hall door.

"I'm on my way to the store for Mom," Doug called. Then he stopped and stood on the ground, straddling the bike pedals and leaning against the seat. "Gee, Rod, aren't you afraid the Witch of the North'll put a spell on you?"

Rod gave his head a little jerk backwards. "Naw," he said proudly. "You know I don't believe in spells, or witches either." There! He'd told Doug the truth.

He'd told Doug Mrs. North wasn't a witch. He'd been meaning to do it for a long time. He couldn't help it if Doug didn't believe him.

"I'm glad you're gonna have the circus," Doug called back over his shoulder, as he rode away. "I'll get my clown suit ready, and see you tomorrow."

Rod pushed open the hall door to the apartments and blew his whistle softly. Nancy Hanks led him up to the second floor. He knelt down on one knee and let her lick his ear. "Tomorrow's the big day," he said to her. "I'll teach you to jump up on Alexander's back."

All Rod's spare time during the next week was spent making ready for the circus. Both dogs seemed to know something important was going to happen. Angie, Annette, and Janie practiced their dance steps and made signs to put on the backyard fence.

BACKYARD CIRCUS AT TEN

ADMISSION 3 CENTS

COOKIES AND LEMONADE 2 CENTS
SEE THE TRAINED DOGS
SEE THE DANCING GIRLS   LOUD MUSIC

At last the day for the performance arrived. Rod was wearing his bright red sport coat and his black rainboots. He looked every bit like an animal trainer, he thought. Doug looked a lot like Googah in the new clown costume his mother made for him, and the three girls were dressed in their dancing school outfits.

When the boys and girls who'd come to see the circus were all seated in folding card table chairs borrowed from neighbors, Angie turned the volume knob on the record player to "LOUD". She picked *THE WILLIAM TELL OVERTURE* for the trained dog act.

Rod and Doug were in the kitchen keeping Alexander and Nancy Hanks from going out ahead of time in their costumes to play with the children in the audience.

"I'd like to have the dog act last," Rod told Doug, "but I don't think we could keep these dogs in the kitchen that long."

"Yeah," Doug agreed. "Best things should come last."

At the sound of the louder music, the dog trainer and the clown went out on the wide back step. The two dogs were straining at their leashes and wagging their hind ends. Rod blew his whistle and made a "down" signal with his hand. Alexander and Nancy Hanks sat at attention. At least things are going fine up to now, Rod thought. He reached in his pocket and took out a dog yummie. He gave one to each dog, along with a pat on the head.

Doug made the boys and girls laugh by seeming to stub his toe and fall flat on his face. He sat down on the step and pretended to cry. He blew his nose loudly on a big red and white polka dot handkerchief. The audience seemed delighted.

Rod strutted around the yard leading Alexander. Alexander followed, wagging his tail. Rod wished the big collie wouldn't act so friendly. He wished Alexander would act fierce and, maybe, strut a little. Finally, they stopped by the step where Nancy Hanks was waiting. The polka dot ruffle around her neck made her look funny.

Angie stopped the music, and Annette and Janie began to beat on the drums made out of coffee cans with rubber from an old tire inner tube stretched across the tops. The beating grew louder and louder as Rod patted Alexander's back. He blew his whistle, and Nancy Hanks jumped up. The audience clapped, and Rod bowed from the waist. Nancy Hanks and Alexander looked proud, too. Angie started the music again, and Rod led the big collie around the yard. This time, Nancy Hanks was standing on Alexander's back.

The boys and girls clapped, and Doug took the dogs to reserved seats in the audience and they sat in them quietly. With the ruffles around their necks, they looked every bit like circus performers. The boys and girls in nearby seats reached over and patted the dogs on the heads.

Rod introduced the dancing girls. "Ladies and gentlemen," he began, using a circus man's voice. "You are about to see three of the most famous dancers in America perform. The lovely Annette, the beautiful Janie, and my sister, Angie! They will tap dance to a tune called PEGGY O'NEILL."

The girls came out of the kitchen on to the wide back step. The audience clapped. This time, Rod operated the record player. When the dance was over, the audience cheered so long the girls had to dance again.

Somebody began chanting, "We want the clown. We want the clown", and the others joined in. Rod went to sit with the dogs while Doug did hand-springs and stood on his head. The boys and girls clapped loudly.

Somebody began another chant. "We want the dancing girls. We want the dancing girls."

Rod jumped up from his chair. He held the dog's leashes tighter in each fist, and he pressed his lips together. Enough was enough! They'd already had one encore, and so had Doug. It was his circus! "No! No!" he yelled above the chanting. "We won't have any more dancing. It's time for refreshments now."

Suddenly everybody was quiet. They just sat, looking at Rod. A burning began in his neck and spread slowly over his face. He wanted to run, but his feet seemed glued to the ground. Besides, he was holding the leashes.

After a hundred years, he heard Mom say gaily, "Lemonade and cookies this way. Everybody this way."

Rod stared at the ground as the guests moved toward the refreshment stand. Doug began collecting two cents from each one. Nobody seemed to notice when Rod took the dogs into the kitchen. He stood by the sink and watched his circus ending without him. The dogs didn't try to pull on the leashes. They seemed to understand how miserable he was.

Doug came in the kitchen with a glass of lemonade in his hand. He held it out to Rod, but Rod shook his head. He watched Mom say goodbye to the last guest and close the gate.

"You didn't wait long enough, Rod," Doug said. "They were going to give you an encore next."

Rod clinched the leashes tighter in his hands. "Go away, Doug."

"I can't," Doug said. "We have to clean up the backyard. We have to take the chairs back, too. I wouldn't leave you to do all that by yourself. Besides, we have to count the money."

Rod unleashed the dogs. Out the window, he saw Mom and Angie stacking the paper cups, getting them ready for the trash. He was glad Dad wasn't here to see him right now.

✦✦ VII ✦✦

The Accident

Rod and Nancy Hanks understood each other. A soft tone of the whistle, or a tug on the leash brought the little black dog to immediate attention. Rod could guide her by looping the end of the leash loosely over his little finger. Usually, he let her pick the direction she wanted to walk, and tonight it was up toward Mrs. Tripp's house.

Nancy Hanks had become famous, too. One day a priest stopped them on the street. "Is this the Nancy Hanks who can ride on a big collie's back?"

When Rod answered, "Yes", the priest asked, "Are you the boy who trained her?" As Rod answered, "Yes" again, the priest shook hands with him, and he felt very proud.

Dad had been working on the ranch for almost three months now, but it seemed much longer. Rod thought about how glad he'd be when the strike was over, and Dad was home for good.

Nancy Hanks paddled along in the November drizzle wearing her new red and blue plaid raincoat. A raincoat for a dog! What a laugh! She was proud of it, too. The "ham"! The hood that covered her head made her look like the wolf dressed in Red Riding Hood's grandmother's nightcap. Lights of an approaching car made the whole world feel unreal.

Then everything happened at once. Miss Kat appeared from behind a bush and came nose-to-nose with Nancy Hanks. There was an explosive sputter, a sharp yip, and Miss Kat darted across the street in front of the car. Nancy Hanks jerked the leash and gave chase. Rod watched in rigid horror as the headlight beams seemed to cover up the little black dog. Then came the terrible screeching of brakes and a shrill ki-yi from Nancy Hanks.

"Nancy Hanks!" Rod screamed.

The yelping little dog disappeared into the darkness of Mrs. Tripp's yard, and then there was silence.

The driver of the car got out quickly and ran

toward Rod. "I didn't see the dog, son. I honestly didn't. I saw the cat, but I didn't see the dog."

"She jerked the leash right off my finger," Rod said with a sob in his throat. "She came nose-to-nose with Miss Kat, and she jerked the leash right off my finger."

"I have a flashlight," the driver said. "I'll help you find her. She went over this way." He pointed in the direction of Mrs. Tripp's yard.

Mr. and Mrs. Tripp came running out of the house, and so did Mom and Angie. Everyone began looking in the shrubbery for Nancy Hanks but she seemed to have completely disappeared.

Rod blew his whistle softly, but there was no answer. "Nancy Hanks, it's me, Rod. Where are you?"

Rod wiped his wet face on his jacket sleeve. "She won't answer me, Mom. She's dead. I know she's dead."

"Maybe she's just knocked out. I'm glad it's drizzling instead of raining real hard. Blow the whistle again. Go ahead. Blow it," Mom said.

Rod blew the whistle again, and everyone kept quiet and listened. Finally, the sound of a faint whimper came from around the corner of the house. Rod and the driver ran in that direction.

"Here she is, Mom," Rod called. "She's hurt bad, but she's breathing. She's alive."

Mrs. Tripp began running toward her back door. "Wait. I'll get a blanket."

Rod looked up. Mr. Tripp and Mom were on their knees beside him, bending over Nancy Hanks, too.

"Don't move her, Rod. Just stroke her head," Mr. Tripp said. "With the leash dragging behind her, it's a wonder she didn't get pulled under the car wheels. We're lucky."

The next thing he knew, Mr. Tripp was lifting Nancy Hanks on to the blanket Mrs. Tripp had brought. She'd brought a pillow along, too. Mom folded the blanket around the little dog, and put her on the pillow.

"Martha, go call the vet and ask him to be waiting for us. He lives next door to his hospital," Mr. Tripp said.

The driver stepped forward. "I'll take you to the vet's."

"No, I'll go," Mr. Tripp said. "It wasn't your fault, anyway. Rod said she ran right out in front of your car."

"Then, here's my name and address," the driver said. "If the dog dies, I'll buy the boy another one."

"No!" Rod sobbed. "She's not going to die! She's not going to die!"

"Hush, Rod," Mom said. "We'll stop by the apartments. You can go up and get Mrs. North."

"Please let me go to the vet's with you," Angie begged.

Mom shook her head. "There won't be room in the car, Angie."

"I'll wait here," Mrs. Tripp said. "She can go in my place. Call me if you need me."

Mom got in the front seat with Mr. Tripp. She was holding Nancy Hanks in her lap. Angie and Rod got in the back seat. When they stopped in front of the Olsen Apartments, Rod jumped out of the car and ran up to the big hall door. He pushed and pushed before he realized he hadn't turned the knob. Inside the hall, he raced up the stairs to Mrs. North's door. Without thinking, he beat on it with both fists.

"Mrs. North! Mrs. North! Come quick! It's Nancy Hanks. She's hurt bad. We're waiting for you in the car. We're on our way to the vet's."

Suddenly, Rod stopped beating on the door and listened. There was no sound from inside. Would Mrs. North come out? Did she hear him? Nancy Hanks was hurt. She needed to get to the vet's. They'd just have to go without Mrs. North.

As he stood staring, the knob turned, and the door opened. A small figure in a black raincoat stepped out. She kept her head lowered and her face turned away from Rod. The hood of her raincoat was pulled down low.

"Hurry," Rod said.

Mrs. North didn't say a word. She went toward the stairs, almost in a run. As the two of them reached the bottom step, she pulled the hood of her raincoat lower.

When they came to the hall door, Mrs. North stood aside and let Rod open it for her. She went out ahead of him and spoke for the first time when she got to the car. "Give her to me," she said to Mom in a quiet voice. "I'll hold Nancy Hanks."

Mom opened the car door and got out. She let Mrs. North get in the front seat beside Mr. Tripp, and she handed her the pillow with the small blanketed dog on it. Then, Mom got in the back seat with Rod and Angie.

As they turned the first corner, Nancy Hanks whimpered, and Mrs. North cooed to her. "Be quiet, Baby. Don't cry, Nancy Hanks. The vet will take care of my baby. Be quiet, Baby."

Rod felt the tears running down his cheek, but he wasn't crying. He was glad it was dark so nobody could see. "I shoulda held the leash tighter, Mrs. North. I shoulda held the leash tighter."

"Stop, Rod. Stop saying that. She's going to be all right," Mrs. North said softly.

Nancy Hanks cried out again. Mom reached over and put her hand on top of Rod's clenched fist. He unmade the fist.

Nobody said anything on the rest of the trip to the vet's except Mrs. North. She kept speaking to Nancy Hanks every time the little dog whimpered. Once Rod saw Angie lean forward with her head turned side ways, trying to see what Mrs. North looked like. When they passed under the next street light, Rod tried to see her face, too, but she pulled the hood of her raincoat lower.

Outside the vet's, Mr. Tripp helped Mrs. North out of the car. Carrying Nancy Hanks on the pillow, she lead the five of them into the waiting room. The vet quickly took her and the dog into the examining room and closed the door.

There was nothing to do but wait. Rod and Angie sat on either side of Mom on a sofa, and Mr. Tripp sat on a big leather chair. One of the dog patients in the ward of the hospital began a song, and several others joined in on the chorus. In a moment's time, there was a regular dog symphony coming from the back room. Several cats added their soprano voices. Nancy Hanks cried out from the examining room.

The strong antiseptic smell of the hospital tickled Rod's nose. It smelled worse than the antiseptic Mom used in the bathroom when flu was going around. After Nancy Hanks stayed for a while, if she had to stay, she'd get used to the smell. If he were a vet, he'd try to find something to use that smelled better. Rod turned his head sideways and raised his eyebrows as he thought. He might decide to be a vet when he grew up. He might decide he'd rather be a vet than a rancher.

THE ACCIDENT

"When'll your dad be home again, Rod?" Mr. Tripp asked.

"The next time there's ranch business on this side of the mountains," Rod answered, "Uncle Jim said he'd send Dad."

"Let's hope it's soon."

It was nice of Mr. Tripp to bring them to the vet's, Rod thought, but he wished for Dad right now. He wondered what Alexander was thinking, shut up in the house all by himself. He must know something was wrong.

"Nancy Hanks ran right into Miss Kat before she knew it," Rod said to Mr. Tripp. "They'd never been that close to each other before. I tried to make them like each other, but they just wouldn't."

"Miss Kat's a cat, and Nancy Hanks is a dog," Mr. Tripp said. "You have to raise them together from pups and kittens before they'll accept each other."

"Nancy Hanks wanted to walk up toward Mrs. Tripp's so she could bark at Miss Kat. I shouldn't have let her go that way."

"Stop blaming yourself, Rod," Mom said.

Mr. Tripp took his pipe out of his coat pocket and filled it with tobacco from a leather pouch. "Yes," he said.

Rod liked the smell of a pipe. Mr. Tripp blew one big smoke ring, and he blew a little one to go in the center.

"May I?" Angie asked.

"Come on." Then Mr. Tripp turned to Mom. "This is a game Angie and I play every Saturday when she finishes helping Martha."

Angie went to sit on the arm of Mr. Tripp's chair. He blew two smoke rings, one inside the other, and Angie put her finger through the center of the smallest one.

"See, I have a double ring on my finger," she said.

Nancy Hanks cried out in the examining room. Rod shuddered.

"Rod, would you like some rings on your finger, too?"

Rod glanced at the closed door of the examining room. "Thanks just the same, Mr. Tripp. I'll watch."

After what seemed a long time, the door opened, and Mrs. North stepped out. She'd pushed back the hood of her black raincoat, and Rod saw her hair was honey-colored like Angie's. It looked pretty piled up on top of her head. She wasn't old, either. She was about Mom's age. Her eyes were big and blue like Angie's, but her face was scarred and shiny.

She stood for a minute and looked straight at Rod

as if she didn't see any of the others in the room. "She's going to be all right, Rod. It's going to take a long time, but Nancy Hanks is going to be all right." Then she started toward the door. Everyone seemed glued to his seat.

Suddenly, Mrs. North stopped and looked at Rod again. He stood up as if he couldn't help himself, and walked toward her. Mrs. North held out her hand to him, and he caught it in his. The two of them went out of the door together, leaving the others to follow.

✦✦ VIII ✦✦

Invited By A Lady

Rod stopped at the bottom step and looked up the hall stairs toward Mrs. North's apartment. Then, he straightened his shoulders, licked the ends of all ten fingers, and smoothed back his hair. He had never been invited for punch and cookies by a lady.

He took a deep breath and began climbing the stairs. The Saturday morning sun shining through small window panes made a tick-tack-toe board of the floor on the first landing. Rod carefully stepped in the middle square with one polished toe of his best shoes. He was wearing his best suit, too. Mom had ironed his white shirt last night. He was proud he could tie his own tie.

Tomorrow, Nancy Hanks would be home from a week's stay in the hospital, and Mrs. North had invited him to her apartment for punch and cookies. He knocked at the door.

A voice came from the other side of the closed door. "Yes?" "It's me, Rod, Mrs. North."

It seemed a long time before the door opened slowly. Mrs. North stood inside, looking sort of scared. "Come in, Rod." She led him to an old-fashioned sofa. "Sit down," she said. "I'll be back in a minute." She disappeared into the kitchen.

The inside of the apartment was warm and friendly. He sniffed the air. The whole place smelled like that powder Mom put in those little lavender satin pillows she was making for Christmas presents. He liked the smell.

A door opened off the back of the living room on to a glassed-in porch. Rod could see it was filled with plants in pots and boxes. Big ones and little ones. Some were on shelves built all around the porch, and some were on the floor. Maybe the flowers made the apartment smell so good. But why did the halls smell the same way?

The clatter of dishes came from the kitchen. Rod folded his arms. He put his feet flat on the floor and held his knees together. Sitting this way, it was hard not to slump. He shifted himself around and tried putting his hands in his pockets. When Mrs. North returned, he was sitting on the edge of the sofa, his back straight as a board, with the palms of his hands flat on the seat on each side of him.

"You're my first guest in this apartment," she said, "and I'm a bit nervous."

So that was why she looked scared. Rod looked straight into her eyes, and they both smiled.

Mrs. North had brought two tall glasses of punch and a big plate of cookies on a tray. She put the tray on the coffee table in front of Rod. The cookies had chocolate icing on them with a whole pecan on top of each one. He remembered what Mom had told him, and he waited for Mrs. North to spread her napkin on her lap. Then, he spread his napkin on his lap in exactly the same way. He waited for her to take a bite of her cookie, and he tried to take a bite the same size. For the next few minutes, they sat eating and smiling at each other.

"I was wondering," Mrs. North finally said, "if you'd like to help me take care of Nancy Hanks when she comes home from the hospital tomorrow? They put a pin in her leg until the break heals, and you'll have to be very careful with her."

"I will," Rod said. "This week I skated down to the vet's every day to ask about her."

"I know you did, Rod. The vet told me. I didn't

know Nancy Hanks had so many friends until last Saturday night."

"Everyone likes Nancy Hanks," Rod said. "Why she has friends all over the place."

"Friends are nice to have," Mrs. North said, as if she were talking to herself.

Rod took another good sniff of the air.

"You like the smell of lavender?" Mrs. North asked.

Rod straightened. She knew what he was thinking, just like Mom. "Yes. Mom's making some little satin things for Christmas presents. They smell like that. Girls put them in their dresser drawers to make their clothes smell good."

She gestured toward the glassed-in porch. "I grow my own lavender plants, Rod. I dry them, distill them, and make my own lavender oil."

"You grow perfume?" Rod asked, surprised.

"Yes. Would you like to see my flowers in the greenhouse?"

Rod put his glass and napkin on the coffee table and followed Mrs. North into the glassed-in porch. He wasn't interested in the plants, except the lavender, but he tried to listen to their names and be polite. "Why do you want to make your own perfume?" he asked.

"It pleases me to do it," she answered, "and it keeps my hands busy."

Rod thought about how lonesome she must be in this apartment by herself. "What else do you do all day long?" he asked.

"I read, and-and I watch people in the streets." She lowered her head as if embarrassed, then quickly explained, "I enjoy watching people and imagining what they're like, especially the boys and girls. I always watch the boys and girls coming and going to school."

So she did watch them out of her window, but not to put a spell on them. She watched them because she liked them. Do I have news for all the kids! he thought.

Mrs. North led him back into the living room. Rod guessed it was about time for him to go. "What time you want me to come over tomorrow to help with Nancy Hanks?" he asked.

"The vet says I can get her late tomorrow afternoon when he goes in to check on the animals. He said to knock on the front door of the hospital. You come about four and go with Mr. Chaney to pick her up."

Rod brightened. "Sure. But aren't you going along, too?"

Mrs. North looked scared again. "Oh, no," she said, shaking her head. "I couldn't. You see, I just couldn't. You'll go for me, won't you, Rod?"

"I'll go," Rod said. "Do you think Nancy Hanks'll ever be able to ride on Alexander's back again?"

"Ride on Alexander's back? Who is Alexander?"

"Alexander's our big collie dog. I taught Nancy Hanks to ride on his back. I trained her with this whistle." Rod took the whistle out of his pocket and showed it to Mrs. North. "We had a backyard circus. You should've been there."

Mrs. North opened her eyes wide. "You really trained Nancy Hanks to do that? Come sit down and tell me all about it. Mr. Chaney said you trained her, but to ride on another dog's back well, that's almost unbelievable."

Rod told Mrs. North how he taught Nancy Hanks to jump up on a box, and later to jump up on Alexander's back. He told her about the circus, the clown act, and about the dancing girls.

"So Edward Roderick Baines, Jr., is your name," Mrs. North said, looking at the whistle Rod showed her. "I like the name. It has a good 'ring' to it."

"Do you think Nancy Hanks'll ever be able to ride on Alexander's back again?" he asked again.

"Oh, I'm sure she will," Mrs. North said. "Just as soon as she gets well."

"Then we could have the circus over again, and you could come," Rod suggested, excited.

Mrs. North put her fingers over her mouth and looked scared again. "Oh, no," she said. "I-I couldn't come to a circus."

"Yes, you could," Rod said so fast the words ran together. "We'd have it right in my backyard. You should see Doug do cartwheels. He's the funniest clown you ever . . ." Rod stopped talking because Mrs. North was shaking her head. "I'm sorry. I forgot," he said.

Mrs. North straightened her shoulders and took a deep breath. "Tell me more about Doug."

"Doug's my best friend. I could bring him up sometime, if you want to see him."

Mrs. North shook her head again and held her hands tightly in her lap. "Not right away, Rod." She looked at her watch. "It's ten o'clock. You'd better go see Mr. Chaney. He has a job he wants you to help him do. That is, of course, if you want to help him."

Rod saw that she wanted him to go. "I need the job. I pay for Alexander's food."

Mrs. North looked puzzled. "You pay for Alexander's food?"

"Yes," Rod said. "Dad's on strike, and he doesn't make much money working on the ranch. He wanted me to let him take Alexander to the ranch, but I'm paying for his food so he can stay here. Alexander wouldn't like being away from me."

Mrs. North smiled. "I'm sure he wouldn't."

✦✦ IX ✦✦

A Day's Work

Rod said goodbye to Mrs. North and ran toward Mr. Chaney's open door. The old man was bent over his desk writing checks. "You wanted me to help you?"

"Yes, Rod. I'd like you to help me take this paint . . ." Mr. Chaney looked around at Rod. He took off his glasses and raised his eyebrows. "I was looking for a working man, though, not a city dude. That's a mighty fine outfit you have on, so you'd better go home and change your clothes. Tell your mother I'd like you to help me all afternoon."

"Mrs. North invited me up for punch and cookies. That's why I'm dressed this way. I'll go home and change."

"How soon do you think you can be back?" Mr. Chaney asked.

"Mom won't let me wear my skates on my best shoes, so I'm walking today. It'll take me a little longer, but I think I can be back in half an hour."

"Good boy. And, Rod, ask your mother if you can have lunch with me. I hope you like beans."

"I like beans fine," Rod said, and he went out the back hall door of the apartments.

As he walked the four blocks home, Rod thought it'd be almost like going out in the boat with Dad. He and Dad always ate beans when they were out on the water by themselves. Rod could almost smell the salt air. He could almost hear the waves sloshing against the side of the boat. They'd buy another one, Dad promised. Rod trusted Dad, no matter how bad things got to be.

At home, Alexander met him at the door. The house was quiet. Rod called several times before he found Mom's note on the dining room table. She'd be back by noon. Angie was at Mrs. Tripp's.

Rod felt lonesome, but he was glad nobody was home. They'd want to hear all about his visit with Mrs. North, and he had to get into his working clothes. He turned the page of the note pad and wrote a note of his own. If Mom didn't want him to stay for lunch or help Mr. Chaney all afternoon, she could call him to come home.

Blue jeans, an old plaid shirt, and his sneakers. Yes, he was ready for work. He patted his whistle to be sure it was in his shirt pocket. Then he put on his jacket. Alexander whined a little when he found he wasn't going along.

"Mom'll be back soon," Rod explained. "We have a big week ahead of us, boy. Dad'll be home, and we'll take you with us everywhere we go. You'll like that, won't you?"

Alexander seemed to understand. He sat down on his haunches on the living room floor to wait impatiently for somebody else to come home. Rod wished he didn't have to go, but he'd promised Mr. Chaney.

Back at the apartments, Mr. Chaney looked at Rod over his glasses and smiled. "Now, you're dressed like a working man. I'd like you to help me take this paint and step ladder up to the empty apartment. It's number seven, at the back. It has to be redecorated before the new tenant moves in. I need you to hand me things while I paint. My rheumatism's been bothering me a lot lately, and it's hard for me to move around very fast."

In a year or so, Rod thought, as they carried the

paint and ladder up the back stairs, he'd be old enough to help Mr. Chaney paint, not just hand him things. He remembered reading how Tom Sawyer hated to whitewash the fence. He couldn't understand why Tom hated to paint so much. Why, painting was more fun than anything.

"Let's put the paint on that old card table I set up, Rod," Mr. Chaney said, "and spread those newspapers on the floor. Cleaning up paint spots is a job I don't 'cotton to' very much. Even latex paint like this is hard to clean up, once it gets dry."

Rod spread the newspapers while Mr. Chaney pried the lid off the can of paint.

Rod wanted to say something. Finally, he sat down on the floor and hugged his knees. Sitting this way made it easier to begin talking.

"Mr. Chaney."

"Yes, Rod."

"Do you know why Mrs. North's face is all scarred that way?"

"Yes, I do, Rod. Hand me that trim brush, will you boy?"

Rod handed him the brush and waited.

"She was burned in a fire," Mr. Chaney said.

Rod thought for a minute. "Why didn't she go to a doctor and have her face fixed?"

"You mean a plastic surgeon?"

"I guess that's what you call them," Rod said.

"You see, Rod, it was her husband who saved her, and he was so badly burned he didn't live. She said she had no right to be beautiful anymore, so she shut herself up in that apartment. I've been trying for years to get her to come out. It looks like it took a boy and a dog to do the job."

Rod watched the old man shake his head slowly. He wondered why Mr. Chaney was so worried about Mrs. North. "How do you know so much about Mrs. North?"

Mr. Chaney looked puzzled. "Didn't you know, Rod? She's my niece. I arranged for her to buy these apartments, and I came here with her to take care of her business affairs. She needed somebody. I was living alone and planning to retire pretty soon, anyway."

So that was why Mr. Chaney was always writing checks, Rod thought, as he watched the old man pour a little of the paint into an aluminum tray and pick up the roller. He had to pay all the bills for the apartments, and he had to pay Mrs. North's bills, too.

"Now, watch me, Rod. You see, I push the roller forward and then pull it backward through the paint. Will you do this for me while I'm up on the ladder? Getting up and down is hard for me to do."

"Sure," Rod said.

Mr. Chaney beamed. "Good boy," he said, and he painfully grunted his way halfway up the ladder. "Now, hand me that roller."

For the rest of the morning, Rod filled the roller with paint and kept the pan filled. Mr. Chaney said a good helper didn't have to be told what to do more than once.

The only paint Rod spilled landed on the newspaper, so that was all right. As they worked, they talked about boats and fishing. About Dad being on strike. About the bicycle Rod couldn't have for Christmas. They talked about Alexander and Nancy

Hanks, about the ranch, and about the backyard circus.

Suddenly Mr. Chaney gave out a long whistle. Rod was tired, too.

"You hungry, boy?"

"Yes," Rod said.

A few minutes later, they were feasting on cold beans, sardines, cheese, and crackers. There was plenty of milk to drink, and an apple for each of them for dessert.

Mr. Chaney pointed to the lanyard around Rod's neck. "You make that?" he asked.

"In cub scouts last summer," Rod answered. "I use it to carry my whistle." He took the lanyard from around his neck and handed the whistle to Mr. Chaney. "It's magic."

Mr. Chaney turned the whistle over in his hand, examining it carefully. "Ummm," he said. "Edward R. Baines."

"That's my Dad's name. Mine's the same. The R. stands for Roderick."

"Nice thing to have, a whistle," Mr. Chaney said. "Why do you say it's magic?"

"So many good things have happened to me since I've had it," Rod told him. "Right after Dad gave it to me for my birthday, my teacher picked me to lead the games at school because I had a whistle. I take Nancy Hanks for her walks, and I make enough money to pay for Alexander's food. I trained the dogs for the backyard circus, too."

Mr. Chaney handed the whistle back to Rod. "Yes, I suppose it is magic, Rod," he said. "Anything is magic if the owner makes it so."

"What do you mean?" Rod asked.

"I mean," Mr. Chaney said, "that you're a dependable boy and a good worker. I'll bet you're a good leader, too. The whistle's magic because you make it so."

Rod looked down at the table and fidgeted in his chair. "Yes, but everybody says I always want to boss everything."

Mr. Chaney cleared his throat. "Do you think you always want to be the whole cheese?"

"Yes," Rod answered, looking up in the old man's face.

Mr. Chaney pushed his chair back from the table. "Then that's something you'll have to work on. Let's go upstairs. I'll clean up these dishes tonight."

Rod sat back in his chair and rubbed his stomach. He felt better. He put the lanyard around his neck and the whistle back in his pocket. "Mom always says, 'At least, let's take the dishes back to the kitchen'."

A few minutes later, they were back at work. They talked about Mrs. North and how lonesome she must be in that apartment all day by herself. Maybe some of the big boys had seen her in the backyard of the apartments when she took Nancy Hanks out at midnight, Mr. Chaney said. The sight of her in her black hooded-raincoat in the shadows was enough to scare the wits out of any kid with a good imagination, Mr. Chaney said. He was sorry the neighborhood was losing a perfectly good witch, but he thought the kids'd like Mrs. North, once they got to know her. He explained he was glad Rod had told everyone why he didn't think Mrs. North was a witch, and he was glad now Rod could tell them he knew she wasn't a witch.

Finally, Mr. Chaney said, "I think we'll stop for today. After you take care of Nancy Hanks on Monday afternoon, I'd like you to help me again."

"I'll be here," Rod said.

Mr. Chaney remarked, "I brought Nancy Hanks home one night in my pocket," he said. "She was asleep when we got here, and she didn't want to be disturbed. She gave out a long wail when I took her out to give her to Wanda. The pocket must've been real warm and cozy." He began adjusting the windows so enough air would get into the apartment to take out the paint smell.

He jerked to attention when Mr. Chaney exclaimed, "Wanda!"

Rod turned around. Mrs. North was standing in the doorway. "I see you two are stopping for the day," she said. "You must be hungry. Come by my place for a snack." She turned and went back down the hall.

Mr. Chaney put his hand on Rod's shoulder. "You know something, Rod? You're what's magic. That's the first time in ten years she's been out of that apartment in the daytime, even in the hallway. If you stay around, she'll be walking Nancy Hanks herself, up and down the streets. Then, you'll be out of a job. But don't worry, there'll always be work for you around here."

✦✦ **X** ✦✦

Christmas

Rod folded the small step ladder, set it against the wall, and stood back to admire the tree. It was December 24th. Dad was gathering up the boxes the Christmas tree decorations had been stored away in, and Mom was vacuuming the rug. Angie was setting up her snow scene under the tree.

"Put the ladder in the garage, Rod," Dad said. "We're almost ready to turn on the tree lights."

As long as Rod could remember, the family had stood together to see the tree lights turned on and to wish each other a Merry Christmas. This year, it was a specially happy time because Dad was home for good. The strike was over, and the men were going back to work at the plant right after Christmas.

"Ready?" Mom asked, and she turned on the switch.

"Merry Christmas!" everyone said at once. Rod hugged Mom, and Angie hugged Dad. Then Mom and Dad hugged each other. They kissed, too.

"It's been a hard pull, Sweetie, but the strike's over," Dad said to Mom.

"Somehow, I can't remember a thing about it right now," Mom said.

"You're my girl," Dad said, patting her on the back.

"May I go now, Mom?" Rod asked.

Mom shook her head. "Not quite yet, Rod. Angie has a treat for us." She straightened Googah in the small rocking chair beside the tree where Angie'd put him, his puppeteer strings still attached.

To Rod, a treat meant something to eat, so he was surprised when Mom walked over to Angie's record player. The music started, and he recognized the tune. It was *THE DANCE OF THE SUGAR PLUM FAIRY*.

"Ready, Mom?" Angie called from the hall.

"Ready," Mom said, and Angie danced in, wearing her circus costume. She twirled and turned, trying hard to stay on her toes.

Rod fidgeted as he watched the rest of the dance.

When it was over, he asked. "May I go now, Mom?"

The door bell rang. It was Doug. He held out a box to Dad. "Here's some cookies Mom sent, Mr. Baines."

Dad held the door open, and Doug came inside. For a minute he just stood and looked at the tree. "It's a pretty one, all right. I wish I had an uncle who owned a ranch."

Angie showed him the lavender satin elf filled with cotton and sachet powder Mom had made to hang on the tree. "Smell it," she said. "Go ahead and smell it."

Doug took a sniff and looked at Rod. "It smells like Mrs. North's dried lavender plants, doesn't it?"

"The elf's the only new decoration we have this year. Mom always buys one special new decoration every Christmas. This year, she had to make it, on account of the strike and all," Angie said.

"I like it better than the bought ones," Doug said, and he took another sniff of the elf.

Angie carefully hung the elf back on the Christmas tree by its hanger made out of red ribbon. "See," she said to Doug. "the branches of the tree are real thick. Dad said he picked out the prettiest tree on the ranch."

Doug stood and looked a little longer. "Well, I

have to go now. I've an errand to do for Mom. You coming down to see my tree this afternoon, Rod? We'll horse around or something."

"That's for sure," Rod said.

Doug rode away on his bike, and Rod watched him until he gave his hand signal and turned the corner. Mom said Christmas was a time for family and friends, and he guessed she was right. He was surprised to discover he wasn't jealous of Doug's bike today, even though he knew he wasn't going to get one for another whole year.

As he closed the door, he turned to Dad and said, "Christmas is a time for liking people you like better than you generally do, huh, Dad?"

"Let's have that again," Dad said, wrinkling his forehead and smiling at the same time.

"Christmas is a time for liking people you like better than you generally do," Rod repeated.

Dad laughed and put his arm around Rod's shoulders. "It's a good thing Christmas never misses a year," he said, and they walked toward the kitchen where Mom and Angie were making lunch.

"I guess I'll have to wait until after lunch, huh, Mom?" Rod asked.

"Yes," she said, "but we can eat right now."

As they ate their soup and sandwiches, the telephone rang. Dad got up from the table and answered it. "When?" he asked. "This morning? Hold it a minute, will you, Jim?" He motioned for Mom to come to the phone. "Tee had the baby this morning," he said. "Here, you talk, Sweetie. Jim isn't making much sense to me."

Mom took the phone. "Hello, Jim. Is it a boy or girl? Boy? Now, just a minute, Jim. Begin again and talk slowly. Did you say boy or girl? Oh, boy and girl? Twins? How wonderful! The first time around being a father, and you get twins for Christmas!" Mom turned to Dad. "Twins, Ed. They had twins!"

Dad laughed. "I heard you. I heard you. I believe you're as excited as Jim. Tell him to take pictures of them for us. We can't afford a trip right now."

Mom turned back to the phone. "You heard what Ed said, Jim? We'll look for some pictures in the mail very soon. We'll miss you for Christmas Day, but we can see you'll have more important things to do. Give our love to Tee."

"Christmas babies," Mom said. She walked back and sat down at the table. "How wonderful."

Rod hadn't left the table when the phone rang. He was hurrying to finish eating. "I've finished my lunch," he said. "May I go now, Mom?"

"Where's he so all-fired bent on going?" Dad asked Mom.

"I told him last night he could invite Mrs. North

and Mr. Chaney for Christmas dinner. Jim and Tee decided last week not to try to come."

"Good idea," Dad said.

Rod put on his jacket and walked out of the house. Alexander followed him to the living room to get his goodbye pat on the head.

The December air was crisp, and the cold reached down to the pit of his stomach, as Rod skated to the apartments. Somehow he had to get Mrs. North to come for Christmas dinner. Christmas was a time to be with friends, and weren't Mrs. North, Mr. Chaney, and Nancy Hanks his best friends, next to Doug? He climbed the familiar stairs, keeping his fingers crossed. Hadn't Mrs. North invited Doug to come along for punch and cookies just last week? Didn't she bring Nancy Hanks to the door each day now instead of looping her leash over the knob? If Mrs. North could come out in the hall of the apartments in the daytime, why wouldn't she come to his house for Christmas dinner?

When he knocked, Mrs. North came to the door. She was wearing an apron, and she had a daub of flour on her face like Mom had sometimes.

"Come in, Rod. I'm making Christmas cookies. Nancy Hanks is in the kitchen with me."

Nancy Hanks came hobbling to the door. Rod

knelt down and let her lick his ear. She was getting better fast, and she was beginning to wag her whole hind end again. She looked funny with a stiff leg, wagging her hind end.

"Just before three-thirty every day, she gets her leash and brings it to me, but you're early today," Mrs. North said over her shoulder, as she walked toward the kitchen to get the leash.

"I didn't come to take Nancy Hanks for her walk," Rod said. "I came to ask you something. I'll be back later for the walk."

Mrs. North stopped and turned around. "You came to ask me something?"

"To eat Christmas dinner with us at my house," Rod said.

Mrs. North drew a short breath. Before she could say no, he hurried to add, "I'm going to ask Nancy Hanks and Mr. Chaney, too. It wouldn't be any fun without them."

Mrs. North stood and looked at Rod.

"Dad brought a big turkey from the ranch. Uncle Jim and Aunt Tee can't come because Aunt Tee had twins this morning. We need you to have dinner with us. Mr. and Mrs. Tripp are going to be there. You know Mr. Tripp. He drove us to the vet's that night."

"Please say yes, Mrs. North," Rod begged. "Alexander'll be gentle with Nancy Hanks. Alexander took care of her real fine at my house the other day."

"I'll be glad to come. I'll get Uncle John on the phone, Rod, you can ask him from here. I want to know what he says."

"Mr. Chaney'll come," Rod said. "I know he will."

Rod waked Christmas morning to the sound of music. Angie must be playing her record player. Mom never had the radio that loud. He was glad it was Christmas Day, but he wasn't in a hurry to get up. He knew what was wrapped in those packages under the tree. Angie and he'd be getting the clothes they needed. Mom had talked about that. Next Christmas it'd be different. When he opened the big square box with the red bow of ribbon on it, he'd probably find a sweater and some shirts. Maybe some socks. When Angie opened the big longish box with the gold bow of ribbon on it, she'd probably find the white raincoat she'd been wanting, and a dress. Maybe a skirt and sweater, too.

Rod was warm under the covers, and Alexander was still asleep in his bed in the corner. Not much use to hurry and get dressed. Rod wiggled his toes, and settled down for a few more minutes snoozing and private thinking. Now, the music was louder. He put his head under the covers. There was a knock on his door.

"Aren't you ever going to get up?"

It was Angie. Angie almost never called him to get up.

"Mom said for you to get up, Rod," she called again, as she knocked on his door a little harder than before.

"Be there in a minute," Rod answered.

By this time Alexander was awake and was trying to open the bedroom door. Rod helped him turn the knob, and then slowly began to dress. He heard Angie and Alexander go down the steps together.

"Rod, boy," Dad called from the foot of the stairs, "I'll expect you up, bright-eyed and bushy-tailed, within five minutes. This is Christmas Day."

Rod stepped out of his bedroom door, fully dressed. "Here I am, Dad." He yawned and stretched and sniffed the delicious smell of roasting turkey.

Mom was standing in the kitchen door. "Hurry, dear. Come down and get washed up. We're about ready to open the presents."

Halfway down the stairs, Rod saw it. Parked in front of the tree, leaning against its kick-stand, was a red English bike with gleaming chrome handlebars and fenders.

Rod's heart seemed to stop and turn a somersault, and his legs felt weak. His throat was dry, and he couldn't say a word. Mom, Dad, and Angie watched him walk slowly down the rest of the stairs, holding on to the bannister. A bike? For him? It couldn't be. He must be dreaming. Maybe he'd wake up in a minute, but before he did, he wanted to touch it. He walked over to the bike and reached out his hands. He ran them gently over the shiny handlebars. He touched the leather of the seat and ran his fingers over the back fender.

No one said a word until Angie asked in a sad little voice, "Don't you like it, Rod?"

Rod nodded.

"I know it isn't new, but see? It has a light, and a speedometer and a gearshift, and hand brakes, and everything."

"It looks new," Rod managed to say. He picked up the card tied to the handlebars with a green ribbon. It said *TO ROD FROM ANGIE WITH LOVE.*

"From Angie? But how—?" Rod almost yelled.

"Mom and Dad bought new tires and tubes," Angie said. "And Dad put them on last night. It was a lot of work."

Mom touched Angie on the shoulder. "But it was all your idea." She turned to Rod. "You remember,

Rod, the bike Mr. Tripp bought for exercise. When he began playing golf, the bike gathered dust in the garage. Mrs. Tripp said Angie could have it for you for Christmas if she'd help out on Saturdays this fall."

Rod looked at Angie. She was waiting for him to say something, but he couldn't. How could a guy be so stupid? He hadn't even bought her a Christmas present. Why didn't Mom tell him about the bike?

For the first time ever, he wanted to give Angie something, something special, but he didn't have any money. He started to hold out his hands to her, but he stopped himself. The hands were empty. What could he do? What could he give her?

THE WHISTLE! Angie'd always wanted it. He'd give her the whistle. He took it out of his pocket and lifted the lanyard from around his neck. Then he reached out, caught Angie's hand, and pressed the whistle inside it.

Angie shook her head. "No, Rod. No."

"I want you to have it. I want to give it to you," Rod said. "It's magic, you know. And you can ride my bike any time you want."

Angie pressed the whistle between the palms of her hands and laid her cheek against them.

"To Angie, from Rod, with love," Mom said softly.